# Read*ux*

Readux Books: Series 6, No 20
Copyright © Joanna Walsh 2015

ISBN: 978-3-944801-38-4

Cover illustrations by Dominik Fraßmann
Cover graphic design by Geoff Mak
Interior graphic design by Susann Stefanizen

Published by Readux Books
Sorauer Str. 16, 10997 Berlin, Germany

www.readux.net

# Grow a Pair
## 9 1/2 Fairytales About Sex
*Joanna Walsh*

*'Il n'y a pas de rapport sexuel'* – *Jacques Lacan*

## I. The Girl and the Penis-Bush

A girl passed a penis-bush growing in someone else's garden, and picked a ripe dick because she couldn't resist it. It came off easily in her hand. She took it home and tried it on right away, knowing that, like the peas in her icebox ('from field to frozen in under one hour!') it would be better fresh. At its base was a thread fitting, the sort you get on a light bulb. It was surprisingly easy to screw in. She gave it a twang. It seemed securely fixed, and bounced up and down agreeably.

Big, swinging dick, she thought. Then, being busy that afternoon, thought no more of it.

At work next day, she had a secret. They say dick-owners think about sex every seven seconds, but it could have been the novelty. In any case it made dull meetings tolerable. She made several unnecessary trips to the bathroom just to look at it, pulled it out like a cowboy, quick on the draw, hung a hand towel on it, peed standing up. She seemed

5

to be able to do this either way as the penis fitted neatly over her clitoris and, when she touched it, felt sort of similar. She wondered if she was in the right bathroom but when she tried the men's she left, overcome by a similar unsettling feeling.

It was only when she was on the tram home that she realised what had been bothering her: she would have to tell her girlfriend she had a dick. As they made salad together, she rehearsed the words, 'Susana, I have a penis,' and the dick jigged a little in her pants, in anticipation.

When the moment came, Susana took it, gingerly, and lifted it, studying the ridge down its underside. When it jumped in response, she dropped it and said, 'Just because I'm touching it doesn't mean I like men,' and the girl felt she had to reply, 'Just because I have a dick now, doesn't mean I am a man. Or that I want to, you know, with it, with you,' though, now that she had a penis, she knew that last part was definitely a lie.

As they set the table, the dick rested in a state of semi-hardness: interested, but waiting for the real action. The girl noticed Susana was texting and leaned over her shoulder.

'"My girlfriend has a dick"? What? Did you put that on Twitter?'

'People put all kinds of crap on Twitter,' said Susana. 'They'll just think it's a joke.'

But minutes later the girl noticed Susana was doing it again.

'I'm just texting Carla,' she said. 'I've known Carla for years.'

Susana didn't stop texting.

So the girl asked her for the third time: 'What now?'

'I said Carla could come round and see it.'

'And what did she say?'

'She's on her way.'

It turned out Susana had not only invited Carla, but also Ida, Alyssa, Carey and Grace. The girl was too shy to show them her dick all at once, so she went in the bedroom and drew the blinds, switching on the dim little lamp on the bedside table and, one by one, her friends came through the door alone.

But the penis bashfully shrank until it was small as a toe, and flaccid as an empty condom. Nothing could be done with it. Grace watered it with the mini-can the girl used for houseplants, Ida warmed it with her breath, Carey read to it from an inspirational text the girl kept on her nightstand, and Carla reprimanded it. Alyssa was last. The girl had always thought she could talk to Alyssa, or that Alyssa could talk to her, or give her advice at any rate. She told Alyssa she was worried that Susana might have invited everyone over because she was unable to face the penis alone.

'Don't be such a dick,' said Alyssa. 'You're acting like a complete cock. Why should anyone else be unable to cope just because you have a penis?' The girl apologised, because she knew it was true.

When she got out, the girl found that Carla, Ida, Alyssa, Carey and Grace had opened a bottle of wine and were eating the salad, as well as some olives that Ida had brought with her, and that Susana was suggesting they call for pizza. Ida was grumbling because so many of the best pizza places had closed down recently but Grace was already dialling and requesting spicy hot. The conversation had moved on from the dick to Carey's application for tenure, and then Alyssa was telling some story about one of her patients which is the sort of thing she does all the time despite her hypocritic oath.

Suddenly the girl was cross, feeling a special kind of rejection that only penis-owners feel. While her friends ate, she sulked in a corner, and didn't laugh at any of the jokes about pepperoni. She sensed that Susana was giggling artificially, that she was nervous. For a weeknight, everyone went home pretty late.

When the girl got into bed Susana rolled over to the extreme limit of the mattress and wrapped herself in the sheet. She must have been balanced right on the edge. The dick pointed toward her, magnetised, and for a while they said nothing until finally Susana spoke.

'You know that I won't,' she said.

'Not even once?'

'No,' said Susana. 'Not even once.'

And the girl, and her penis, turned sadly away.

## II. The Three Big Dicks

Just to the east of the city where Susana and the girl lived was a forest, and in the forest there lived three big dicks. The first dick was tall and straight, the second was long but bent slightly, like a banana – which some people found amusing, and others, exciting – and the third was squat but made up in girth for what it lacked in height.

The three dicks lived together in a little wooden house, and they were always looking for pussy.

But very little pussy came by their neck of the woods, which was unsurprising as they lived so far off the beaten track. Finally, the tall dick said to the short dick, we must make our own pussy, and the bendy dick said, good idea, but what could we use?

The first, tall dick decided to construct a pussy from matchsticks. It took a long time, during which he never left the house. When it was finally finished it was an impressive edifice, though in use it was rough even when lubricated. He could not

10

understand why the perfect thing he had made gave him so little pleasure.

The third dick, the short, thick one, knew he could do better. He bought many, many packets of Jell-O from the nearest grocery store, which took him several days to reach, partly due to the remoteness of the forest house, and partly due to the dick's lack of legs, which meant he couldn't get about very quickly. As he paid, the third dick noticed the assistant who fumbled the packets. She was unsure what to do, seeing a dick in the shop; perhaps she should call the manager. Now she was pussy, thought the third dick, and she looked cute when she blushed and lowered her eyes every time she looked at him. But not that cute. The Jell-O would be better. When the third dick returned to the house in the woods, he mixed the Jell-O as instructed on the packets, and poured it into a mould he had fashioned from a hollow half tree trunk. When it had set and was disgorged, it glistened in the evening sun, a tower of shining pink pussy. None of the three dicks had ever imagined one so big. They whooped and hollered and danced around it and photographed it with their phones until they were exhausted, then it came on to rain and the Jell-O became nothing but a strawberry-scented memory.

The second, bendy, dick thought and thought but, besides matchsticks and Jell-O, he couldn't imagine what else to use. He took a long walk in the woods so he could think some more – weaving at angles between the trees, naturally – until he came to a stream, which he crossed, then a road, which he followed until he reached the very end of the forest. No sooner had he stepped from its shade into a wide green meadow than he met a cunt, which he failed to recognise, never having encountered one before.

## III. The Witch

The cunt the second big dick spotted was also a witch.

The witch had once lived in a castle where she had been not a witch but a queen, and she had been married to a king. All day long they sat, like wooden chess pieces, on matching thrones in the throne room. At the end of each evening they got up, bowed to each other, stiffly, from the hips, then paraded down the length of the room while all the courtiers and commoners marvelled at their perfect synchronicity. Then they went to lie down under wooden sheets between the posts of their wooden four-poster bed.

There was something about the queen that had grown too big. I don't mean her ass, or her tits – though middle-aged, she had no spread – but she had grown into the shape of her long wooden gown, and had become all of a piece with her wooden clothes, filling out their carved drapes and folds until they were were one with her body. This, naturally, prevented her from fulfilling several physical functions. The necessary tasks of waste management were provided for by holes she had secretly bored with an old-fashioned hand drill. She did not make more. It was not that the queen did not like sex, but it involved indignity and the possibility of disrespect. The king, she knew, respected her perfectly, and would never have dreamt of putting her into any undignified position, but pleasure somehow kept getting in everywhere, except into the queen, who kept such a close guard against it. The king, she observed, still seemed able to bend despite his official position, and this apparent flexibility attracted many young girls who admired the way such a kingly person could continue to swerve to the left, and right, and even forward and back again. The queen would invite these girls to tea and explain that she was very concerned that persons of such a young age should be infatuated with someone who was, after all, old enough to be their father, and that it would be far better for them to concentrate on their studies, until, before they knew it, they found themselves wrapped up in a cobweb spun so entirely of the queen's good intentions that they hardly noticed their entanglement. Unable to move or speak, they were hung in their little cocoons on hooks in the key cupboard in the butler's pantry.

The queen had seen off so many young girls. It was becoming exhausting. And, besides, there was only one hook in the key cupboard left unused.

One day someone appeared at court, whom the queen refused to think of as either male or female, so that she did not have to acknowledge this person's extraordinary sexual attraction. The queen was bored, and the king had left her alone in the palace, as usual, so she invited this person in to tea. If things get out of hand, she thought, there is always the butler's pantry.

'Did you ever wonder why the king never takes you anywhere?' asked the person as soon as s/he sat down, which was really quite forward of (the queen thought, if ungrammatically) 'them'. Before the queen could reply they said, 'It's because you seem to disapprove of everything, and are quite haughty.'

'I am not haughty,' the queen protested, genuinely shocked. 'In fact I am known throughout the realm for my fair-mindedness and easy-going nature.'

'It is true,' said the person, 'that you are easy-going with your people. That is because you believe it is necessary to go easy with them. You believe you must go easy because you are too hard for them. And you are right. You are hard. You are not a queen. You are a witch.'

The queen thought about this for a while, and, because she was an intelligent woman, she realised that the stranger was right. She did not resolve to mend her ways (again because she was an intelligent woman), but to become fully a witch.

How did she do that?

I'll try to think. Perhaps she did it by leaving the king (who, after all, was no more than a common-or-garden adulterer, and, because of the queen's spells, an unsuccessful one at that). Perhaps she did it by taking many lovers. But I think this is unlikely. Perhaps she did it by manipulating the young women who had come within her power, but, no, she really was fair-minded.

Always, in connection with the witch's story, I feel inclined to make judgements. As I am not at all a judgemental person, this is very strange, but, a witch is a witch, and her influence is strong. Perhaps she can exert herself, even through words on paper. I would not be surprised if she was a very powerful witch indeed, always judging: good or bad, right or wrong, even without knowing it, even when asleep.

So I'm not sure how to get my witch out of her predicament. She is simply too strong for me. She is like a frozen princess only slightly less beautiful, which I in no way hold against her. All I know is that she was once a queen living in a castle, and now she is a witch living in suburbia. She seems satisfied with her lot, so, instead of going on, I will start another story.

## IV. The Waiter and the Laundress

Back in the city a little while before all this, a man and a woman were attracted to each other but, lacking both primary and secondary sexual characteristics, had nothing with which to express their desires.

The woman, who happened to work in a laundry, stole a bra, put it on, and stuffed a T-shirt into each cup, then placed between her legs an inside-out sock, sewing a pearly shirt button to the top of the opening that protruded from between her thighs. The man, who waited tables in a restaurant, took dumplings from a stew that was cooking in the kitchen and, in between them, set a large, stiff potato peeler. Thanks to this paraphernalia everything went swimmingly until one day the woman noticed that the sock was wearing thin and, due to the attentions of the potato peeler, was already frayed in several places. Moreover, her lover had begun to request that she replace the single sock with an inverted pair of tights which sounded, at best, uncomfortable and, at worst, a sign that he no longer found her sock alone enough.

'I'm afraid deep down, that he wants to hurt me,' she told her therapist.

'How does that make you feel?' asked the therapist who, herself, relied on a narrow length of rubber hose and, her husband, an overripe banana.

The man, meanwhile, questioned his potato peeler. For a while he replaced it with a corkscrew, then a battery-powered cappuccino-frother, then an egg whisk, and finally a power drill. He plucked up the courage to consult a friend. They went to the bathroom together in an entirely innocent manner, as they were in a bar that wasn't at all that sort of bar, where the waiter got out his power drill feeling half-proud, half-ashamed. 'Not the latest model. You should try the 5.2,' his friend said, flashing his.

The waiter and the laundress did not mention these encounters to one another, neither wanting the other to think they were too inexperienced to have known that this sort of thing went on all over the city, as indeed it did, between mangoes and wooden spoons, slippers and umbrellas, purses and boot shapers, as well as between matching duos of German sausages, and pairs of differently topped fresh donuts.

Still the waiter was never satisfied. And the laundress was never satisfied.

'All I want,' he said, 'is to feel adequately authentic.'

'All I want,' she said, 'is to feel that I am enough.'

So together they began to create an enormous machine in which every object that could conceivably be put inside anything else was inserted in every possible combination; where all things that could be frotted were rubbed together, moistened by a thousand different liquids of various viscosities; where anything soft had its corresponding squeeze, where anything that could be pulled, sucked, spanked or bit was answered by a clamp, vacuum, switch or set of mechanical teeth. For a small fee any inhabitant of the city could add his or her appendage to the machine and watch while it satisfied itself in an infinite number of unions. Within weeks all the people in the city hooked up to the mechanism whenever they wanted their sexual needs taken care of, leaving them otherwise free to go about their everyday business. And so it happened that the sex machine became a great success, which was lucky for the man and the woman for, as no one was interested in sex any more, both the restaurant and the laundry went out of business.

## V. The Princess and the Penis

News of the sex machine had not yet reached the castle, despite its being in the centre of the city. In addition to the king and, until lately, the queen, in the castle there lived a princess who was always looking for a proper cock.

She was often texted pictures of cocks by her male acquaintances, but it was difficult for her to gauge what they might be like in the flesh. The screen on her phone was so small, and besides, she was well aware that her male friends might be trying to impress her: after all she was a princess. All the cocks she was sent pointed straight up, some at a slight angle, and others with some kind of bend, either up towards the belly of the owner, which she liked, or over like a tap, which she liked less. Some were nicely rounded, and others had tactile facets. But she had a feeling someone was playing a trick on her: how did they stand up without any help, which, she thought, was surely physically impossible? Due to the splendid isolation guaranteed her by her social position she had never met a cock IRL and, as there was no Wi-Fi in the palace, she had no opportunity to check the facts.

She was waiting for her one true cock, but none of the cocks in the photos seemed to fit. She wanted one that would fit like a glove, or rather like the finger of a glove which she used on herself while waiting for the proper cock to arrive. It was not her glove, naturally. She was looking for something more masculine, and more foreign than her own delicate middle finger. The glove was a rough glove – made of suede with external ribbed stitching – that someone had left around the place one time when visiting. She couldn't remember whose it was, but it was definitely a man's glove, and one day she got the idea that if she could find the man who possessed the other glove, he would surely have the perfect cock to match. She put an ad in the *Castle Times*, but no matching glove was forthcoming.

In the meantime, she had an idea. She would invite all her male friends to let her play around with their dicks and, when she found the one she liked best, she would go the whole way, and also possibly marry and confer on it half her kingdom. To guarantee fairness by preserving anonymity, she

22

ordered that all the spare mattresses in the palace should be piled on her bed. Each night she would lie on top of the topmost mattress with the cock sandwiched between the two at the bottom. She was looking for a cock that could make itself felt, whatever the circumstances.

Of course the man in question should not be attached to the cock. For one thing, it was possible he'd suffocate under the weight of mattresses. For another, she was a princess, and it wouldn't do for just anyone to know what she did in bed, and make a sex tape, or sell his story to some magazine. Instead, when a guy visited her room, she took the mini guillotine her father used to decapitate cigars and asked him to lay his dick beneath the knife. As she was a princess, not one of them dared to disagree. Afterwards, most hid their distress out of respect for royalty, except for the last who immediately decided he was better off without it, and set off right away on a hunting expedition to a country where he'd heard vaginas still bred in the wild, hoping to bag one for himself. Once off, the penises that had begun their adventure so hopefully erect usually drooped a little. The princess revived them with stroking and kisses, before placing them under the bottommost mattress. But once under her pile of mattresses, the penises were not much good to the princess. Most failed to retain their firm texture. They pointed, sadly, in the direction their owners had taken, and, whimpering quietly, showed little interest in her.

Until one night the penis belonging to the man who was glad to be rid of it bored a hole straight through all of the mattresses until it found her, slipped between her legs and inside her. After a little thrashing, she went to sleep, knowing that this was definitely the proper cock she had been searching for.

When she woke up the next morning, the cock was still in place, so they did the same thing all over again. Once they had finished it didn't seem to want to come out, so she showered and dressed, and went down to breakfast, then to her tennis lesson and her astrophysics class. She found that she could walk about with the penis inside her all the time, and nobody noticed. It was only occasionally that it wriggled so much that it made her twitch, and she had to press her legs tight together to calm it.

For the first few days the princess was happy with the situation. She had sexual pleasure on tap, and the cock was delighted to have finally found a use for itself, its previous owner having had paid it little attention. But the next Thursday the princess was walking in the palace garden with the penis firmly inserted, when she discovered it was a speaking cock. I don't know what it said to her – I wasn't there – but it was something dickish. She shushed it, but it wouldn't shut up. Luckily she was in the middle of an enormous parterre and there was no one else around, until a duchess passed by on the path to the Garden of a Thousand Roses, and the dick called out something profoundly unsuitable. The princess coughed and looked around. There was no apparent source for the words, except her, and, naturally, she didn't want to be accused of behaving like a tool. The cock shouted something even more prickish and the duchess turned to see who could have said such a thing. All the princess could do was clap her hand over her vulva to stifle the noise while the cock wriggled inside her trying to make itself heard.

Once back in her wing of the palace, she asked the penis to come out, but it wouldn't. She cajoled it, threatened it, squeezed it as hard as she could. She tempted it by squatting over fine-art smut taken from the royal picture gallery, but all it would do was shout, 'Fuck you!' as loud as it could, until she had to throw herself onto her bed and cover herself up with some of her many mattresses to prevent anyone from hearing.

The man to whom the penis belonged was, at that time, in another country, far away. During his long journey he had encountered many hazards, fording rivers, climbing mountains and travelling by several budget airlines that had overcharged him for baggage and late check-in. But it had been worth it, for here vaginas of every colour flew from tree to tree, flapping their delicate labial wings above his head as he tried to tempt them into his butterfly net. He had almost caught a juicy specimen when his cell phone rang. It was the princess.

'I have a problem,' she said. 'Your penis is behaving like a dick.'

'It's nothing to do with me any more,' he said. And then he lost signal, and went back to chasing tail. He netted a spectacularly coloured cunt that was hovering over a nearby flower. He slapped it between his legs where his cock had been. It trembled, and fluttered, but stayed in place. To test that it had really stuck, he sucked his finger and gently poked it into the cunt's centre, to find that, yes, it yielded softly until his finger really did fit through its parted wings all the way into his body. The cunt was already wet from the honey it had been carrying.

The princess shut herself into her room and saw no one. Her family, naturally, became concerned. After the queen's disappearance and all the fuss about the king's string of new girlfriends, they didn't want another royal scandal. They advertised, discretely, a massive reward for anyone who could find the reason for the princess's seclusion, and cure her of her desire to be alone, but after the penis-guillotine incidents, few volunteered and those that did were, naturally, not very intelligent. The princess decided to call the cock-owner again.

He took the call as he emerged dripping from the sea. He'd travelled from the forest to the coast, where he had been diving for tits, all varieties of which pulsed semi-transparently through those waters. He strode naked from the ocean, one clasped to either bosom. After only a little while he taught them to lie quiet, and they lay affixed to his chest by their own power of suction. They gleamed and, even on land, preserved a slight translucence, rising and falling gently as though only his heart were beating beneath them (which it was, as tits, like the jellyfish they resemble, are heartless).

'Your cock is beyond a joke,' said the princess. 'I insist that you come back for it right now.'

'But I don't want it,' said the man who was now, to all intents and purposes, a woman.

'It's yours. You can do what you like with it, so long as you get it out of me,' said the princess.

The man, who was now called Linda, sighed, and agreed. After all, he owed the princess one.

It was she who had set him off on his path to transformation.

He took the next plane home.

The princess invited Linda up to her bedroom. They called the penis out, but all it would do was shout, 'Bollocks!' When it noticed Linda and sensed – through her clothing, as dicks can – her large and colourful cunt, and her delicately shimmering and only slightly gelatinous breasts, it changed its tune. 'Hey baby,' it said, 'we should play strip poker. You can strip, and I'll poke you.' The penis clearly no longer recognised its owner. 'Hey girl, did you know the human body has 206 bones,' it yelled, 'and I'm going to give you another!' Linda could now see how her former cock could be a problem. She had an idea. She asked the princess to strip and to press her body against hers. She carefully spread the lips of her butterfly cunt and pushed it against the opening from which she could just see the end of the cock protrude. Linda asked the princess to press tighter and tighter, so the princess wrapped her legs around Linda's waist. The double clitoris-antennae at the top of Linda's butterfly cunt embraced the princess's single clit, until it stood upright and the lips of her cunt swelled, and moistened, and parted, and when she came the cock slid from the princess right into the cunt of its former owner. It went in so deep that its voice was muffled and it caused no further embarrassment to anyone.

So Linda collected a fabulous reward from the royal treasury, and the princess was no longer mortified while fulfilling her public engagements. But the cock would not come out of Linda, who was unable to use her new cunt with anyone but this leftover of her old self. And the princess, once bitten twice shy, went back to using her old leather glove, until it became stiff and shiny, and darkened with use.

## VI. In Another Part of the Forest

There once was a woman who found she could have sex remotely.

She discovered this by accident. She was feeling quite perky and free from love, having recently finished with the finishing of a relationship, and was now onto the finishing with the finishing of it. Each stage was smaller than the last, and each caused her less pain, like descending, or perhaps ascending, a flight of stairs. She was at work when it happened, in her job as an IT Officer at a large company located in a business park set in a woodland glade, and her discovery, though inconvenient, was not unmanageable. She did not have an office, but she did have a cubicle, which was actually more private, as all the offices in her building had glass walls.

It happened like this.

She was writing up a report in which she had to type the word Zoroastrian. This was not a word she had ever had to type before. The Z key on her computer had never been pressed. As soon as her finger hit the letter Z, she could sense that somebody, somewhere on the office's local area network, was coming.

In the canteen at lunch she tried to determine who it might have been. She studied her co-workers to see whether any of them were looking unusually confused, or bashful, or cheerful, or rumpled. She hovered by the counter, pondering whether to have a soup and roll, or the noodle pot and a blackcurrant yoghurt, and many of her co-workers passed by but she still couldn't tell.

In the afternoon, she tried again. She typed zoo, zither, azalea, Zambia, Zola and eurozone, none of which she had found necessary to include in any work communication before. She knew that every time she pressed the Z key, the same thing happened. When she used the shift key, she felt the effect was greater. She could even occasionally hear cries and groans exploding from behind one of the flimsy fibreboard walls.

When she got home she tried the Z key on her own laptop to make sure it wasn't just the work computer, and found that she was right. She knew that, whenever she pressed the Z key, somewhere, she was producing the same effect. Each time she pressed the key, she experienced a mild sensation of sexual pleasure but nothing, she knew, compared to what was going on at the other end.

She eventually stopped working altogether, for the pleasure of randomly stimulating strangers. When she was sacked, it was over something minor. They knew what she'd been doing, she was sure, but they didn't want to bring it out into the open.

Having no money, she was forced to go back and live with her parents. Even there, all she did was continue. By using a proxy server to change her IP address's location, she found she could access people all over the kingdom. Even if they blocked her, she could still get to them.

The day came when she'd had sex with everyone in the entire nation: she'd fucked all the men, and all the women too, some of the domestic animals, and even the houseplants. Her parents tried to encourage her to get a job. She could have used her skills to help those experiencing sexual dysfunction. She could have trained as a sex therapist, or made millions as a self-help guru. She was offered high sums to work for porn studios, but she only wanted to carry on pressing the button until she found her ex-lover and made him come until he possibly died.

## VII. Simple Hans

This morning I had my first ever cup of coffee. It was a very tiny cup, and made me feel like a giant. We were in a coffee shop. He was much younger than me. I knew that, but he didn't. He was a grown up, but a very new one. I have spent a very long time as a young child, much longer than most. I dyed my hair for the occasion, but the chin hairs were already growing on me. They were sharp and tough as pig's bristles. He was nervous. He told me about something called the Internet. I pretended I knew all about it already.

When we went to bed, his limbs were white and speckled. They had too many angles. His cock was a right-angle to mine. There seemed too many of them, always going in and out of something else. Outside the cafe, an old friend of my father's had seen me walking with him, and had shouted, 'cradle snatcher!'. We pretended she was trying to communicate with someone else.

After that we spoke by instant message. He sent me 'who knew cheese exploded?!?!?'

I tried to send him a guinea pig, but it wouldn't go through the screen, though I pushed and pushed.

He wasn't there. The guinea pig remained with me. I tried to put my cock in the screen. It didn't work. It hardly mattered. After what happened to the guinea pig, the pale guy didn't want to see me again.

I tried other things: Grindr, Tinder, OkCupid, but they were all the same. There seemed to be no communication in the world, so I left the town where I was born, as all youngest sons should. It was time for me to go to seek my fortune.

I rented a bedsit in a suburb of a small seaside town. After a week in this new place no fortune arrived. It was winter. The sun slanted quick and narrow across the day. Dark came too soon and I slept. There was not enough daylight for a fortune to appear.

In the meantime I liked to look at the ads in corner shop windows, which made me feel part of this new place, and also allowed me a frisson of contempt for the sellers of second-hand children's clothes, and *Ironing Services*, and *Bums 'n' Tums for Mums*. This is not nice but it's OK: I am not from here and, being lucky, don't have to worry about such things. I saw

Helen's ad in the shop window. On a small card it said, *Victorias Secret Massages for the Discerning.* I thought, I'd have put a semi-colon, or a colon. There wasn't even a full stop. Or an apostrophe. Of course she wasn't called Victoria.

I booked an appointment on the phone. 'What name?' said Helen, who, I had thought, was called Victoria. I said my name. 'He doesn't want to give his name?' said Helen. 'That's OK.' 'It's my name,' I said. 'Yes, I know,' said Helen.

Helen lived in a flat above another shop in the same high street. It sold electrical goods. Or maybe the flat was where she worked. I sat in a room that might have been a waiting room or might have been a living room. There was a floral sofa. She shouldn't have bought such a pale print. No, it was a waiting room, not a front room; there was no direction anywhere, not towards a telly, or a fire-place, or a window. Everything faced in, the chairs not quite towards each other. They nudged each other's corners, tried not to notice. I stared at a patch of wall under a shelf made of stick-on wood-effect vinyl with a pot plant on it.

Helen was wearing a white uniform like a nurse. I could see what she was wearing under-neath, like a comedy nurse, not a real healthcare official. When I took the pale boy to A&E the nurses wore garments like grocery plastic bags in pastel blues and greens, gathered around their wrists and ankles with elastic. They wore jellyfish on their heads, which were also in marine colours. You couldn't tell if they were boy or girl.

Helen said, 'Normally there's me or Isa, but today there's just me. Isa's here on Saturdays, Sundays and Tuesday afternoons. If you want Isa you'll have to book one of those slots. I'm here all the time.' She said, 'How old are you?' She said, 'It's adults only. And usually men.' I said, 'I'm not a woman you know, and I'm not as young as I look.'

She took me next door and I stripped and lay on a hospital gurney on a fresh white towel.

When she had massaged me for a while, I pulled her toward me and she said that wasn't in the deal. She said I'd have to pay extra but frankly no one ever wanted extras – this was a stingy town. And unimaginative: think of all the churches. This is the part in the story when it's normal for youngest sons to resist, or perhaps to give in: I can't remember. Her cunt was dry and unused, having never been part of a deal, ever. I stuck my head between her legs and rubbed my hair into hers causing static electricity. She opened like an iced bread bun, lips forced apart by a whorl of stiff whipped cream – you can buy them in Greggs Bakery on the high street.

It tasted of salt and air, just the same as the cream. They say the sea air's good for you. Or perhaps she had the window open. A little knob of flesh stood out at the top of her cunt. I wanted to bite it, but she pulled back as my teeth snapped closed.

I came again on Tuesday afternoon. I brought her something shiny. This was what the gift guide in the magazine said ladies like. I'd lifted it from the shop where I'd seen her advert. I pulled flowers from gardens as I passed, but Isa was there, not Helen. Isa said, 'Hello my name is Claudia.' I paid, stripped and lay down. She swished her long dyed ponytail over my body. She unbuttoned her nurse's coat and swung out her dumbbell breasts, straddled me and lowered herself so they bulged against my chest. The whole of her was flattened against me like she'd dropped there from the ceiling, like she'd overbalanced, and couldn't get up again. I could feel air between us in the gap underneath her breasts. The rest was sweaty. We unpeeled.

Isa said if I wanted to see her or Helen again I should go away for a long time. I said, should I complete three tasks? The tasks would be hard, I knew. But I am lucky, and in the end they were easy. I came back anyway.

There was a little old man who helped me, and a donkey. I thought it should talk, but it didn't, however I tried to make it. But those bits are for other stories. Like the youngest sons in fairytales, I treated them to what they seemed to ask for, so that when I asked them again they did exactly what I told them to.

In the high street there were lights. On the chimney pot of the flat above the chemist, a Santa, lit from inside, ready to plunge. I walked past the Christmas houses with the lights on, boxes in different shapes, all designed keep something in, or out. You could scream out here and they'd never notice; or maybe they would: it's only bricks and mortar. All those boxes, all close together, all built to be the best shape to capture happiness. Did any of them work?

When I returned to Helen, she asked me to cut off her head, and I did it. Isa held her down and I used an axe from the hardware store where I'd also seen an *Astrology 2005* decorative dish still hopefully for sale. I could have gone for a saw, but it was the axe I lifted for her. I think she was meant to transform but I can't think what into: she was already a woman. I think we were meant to get married or something, after, and that showers of gold would pour from the wound, but nothing happened. Nothing except what you'd expect.

I'm not very good with words. I use them here but often they can't get out. I'm trying to tell you what it was – to cut into this thing that should be sacred, the thing we can't question, to make it just a thing like any other – which is what it becomes when you cut into it, when you cut it off. This is the moment the good things happen in the stories, but this is real life. She was meant to change into something else. But she did. I looked into both of the parts of Helen that were left after, but neither of them answered.

So I didn't get a fortune this time. But I am the youngest son, and a boy. Luck follows me, Simple Hans.

In any case, I'd only come for the week.

## VIII. The World's Greatest Lover

The World's Greatest Lover is a courteous and unassuming gentleman. When greeting a lady, for example, he always kisses her hand, regardless of who she is. The queen, although perhaps the most famous, is by no means the only woman to have received this mark of respect. In return for his politeness local residents allow him to live in comparative peace and will often be uncooperative about directing strangers to his home, despite the fact he can be seen walking or cycling around the city almost daily. No one knows his true identity.

Despite his success, the World's Greatest Lover was not content. Something was interfering with his business. Orgasms – suddenly so common, if unpredictable – undermined his trade. To make someone come, as if at the touch of a button, was not playing fair. The World's Greatest Lover charmed his army of unpaid interns into tracking down the source of the problem, and invited the unemployed

IT Officer to meet him at a swanky restaurant. He arrived heavily disguised in order to prevent public incidents, such as women throwing themselves into the road from the pavement opposite to get to him. For the same reason, though the restaurant was not brightly lit, he wore dark glasses.

The World's Greatest Lover had never felt uncontrollable desire, or jealousy, and this is what made him the perfect date. He had also chosen his venue with unerring judgement. It was the ideal date restaurant: there were all kinds of knives and forks on the tables, and the chef took very fine and fresh ingredients and turned them into something unrecognisable. On arrival he presented the ex-IT Officer with a single red rose. He inclined his head rather stiffly, she thought, as though his chiselled features were indeed made of wood. There was something about him she found familiar.

The ex-IT Officer remembered nothing the World's Greatest Lover said to her over dinner, only the warm effect of his speech, which buzzed through her body and mind simulating the first stages of arousal.

When the World's Greatest Lover suggested a moonlit walk along the clifftop, she agreed. At the spot he had calibrated as most romantic, at that exact moment the moon appeared from behind a cloud, suffusing the landscape with a magical silvery light and glinting off his face like a gold coin. He said, 'Close your eyes.' The ex-IT Officer did as she was told, and he led her on by the hand.

'Can I open my eyes yet?' asked the woman, who had suddenly remembered exactly who he was.

'No,' said the World's Greatest Lover. 'Just a little further.'

He led her right to the edge of the cliff, where he pushed her off.

'OK,' he said, 'you can open them now.'

## IX. The Minutes of a Meeting Between Mrs Darsie Hurlbutt, Hortense Shakely, Raymond Maths and Doctor Maxman, Including a Skype Call from Mrs Gustie Slovak

In the absence of a monarchy, the king and queen both having gone missing, and the princess being unwilling to govern, a council has hastily been formed to address the situation.

Mrs Darsie Hurlbutt, Hortense Shakley, Raymond Maths and Doctor Maxman (who is a woman) assembled for their meeting, and waited for a Skype call from Mrs Gustie Slovak.

Hortense Shakley (who is a man) said, *Wanna get laid tonight?*

Doctor Maxman said, *Make her shiver in ecstasy and desire more!*

Raymond Maths said, *S..A..F_E_ -&_ F-A..S..T.. -- P_E N I S___ -E N..L-A R-G E M-E N_T-*

The meeting was held in the Sarajevo suite of the Balkan Hotel, located on the ring road of the city, in a pale grey room with a dark grey carpet, and a lighter grey conference table. The walls, though they look grey, are in fact off-white. Outside it was snowing. Through the lightly tinted windows the snow, though white, looked grey.

On a steel-effect laptop, a Skype window opened.

Mrs Darcie Hurlbutt (chair) invited Mrs Gustie Slovak to speak.

*Hey guys,* began Mrs Gustie Slovak, *I am very passionate with a very hot lean and curvy physique. I am very hot 36E 26 waist 39 butt. 100% all REAL PHOTOS !!!! Im exactly what u have been looking for Ive got skills like no other! Im very openminded & love role-playing! Cum play me with baby :)*

Mrs Gustie Slovak was a long way off. She wasn't coming through very clearly. Perhaps her connection was not good.

Mrs Darcie Hurlbutt said, *Dearest One, Greetings. With warm heart I offer my friendship and greetings.*

Dr Maxman said, *However strange or surprising this contact might seem to you as we have not meet personally or had any dealings in the past.*

Mrs Gustie Slovak said, *This is a personal message directed to you and for your consideration alone.*

Raymond Maths straightened his tie. He said, *S..A..F_E_-&_ F-A..S..T..-- P_E N I S___-E N..L-A*

44

*R-G E M-E N_T-*

Dr Maxman said, *I NEED YOUR ASSIST-ANCE.*

Mrs Darsie Hurlbutt said, *I don't want to sleep alone any more.*

Mrs Gustie Slovak said, *The World's LARGEST Swinger Personals Community: Unlimited messaging 2-way webcams Access to thousands of sexy member photos and amateur videos First pick of new members Priority customer support 24/7 And much more!*

Raymond Maths said,

HERBAL PENIS PILLS
Click on the Attachment Bell
ow:

Mrs Gustie Slovak said, *you can be sure you are flirting with the real deal who is looking for a man just like you!*

Dr Maxman said, *I am contacting you so that we can agree on the transaction of $9.5,Million. U.S dollars which was left in the bank by my late client who has the same surname with you.*

Mrs Gustie Slovak said, *This is NOT a dating site. You're lucky, free registration for men is open for a very limited time.*

Dr Maxman said, *I am not a man.*

45

Mrs Darsie Hurlbutt said, *I want to invest in your country with you and again in a very profitable venture.*

Mrs Gustie Slovak said, *Click on attachment below.*

They clicked on the attachment and a video window opened. They saw Mrs Gustie Slovak unbutton the tweed-effect business jacket that strained across her waist, then the cream silk-effect blouse that strained across her chest. Underneath, she was wearing a purple lace-effect bra that strained against her E-cup breasts. She must have unhooked it, because out they tumbled only a little less buoyant than they had been in the underwired push-up. Her nipples were large and hard and shaped like babies' dummies. Radiating from their aureoles were stretch marks slightly lighter than the colour of her skin.

All said, *Click on attachment below.*

They clicked, and Mrs Gustie Slovak pulled up her tight business skirt, pulled down her beige lace-effect shapewear, and pushed her thighs hard against the screen so that they bulged against each other. Then she opened out the large purple lips at the top of her thighs and pressed them against the screen and inside was a bright coral colour.

Dr Maxman said, *No Gimmicks. No Bullshit. Just InstaBangers who want to f@ck!*

Mrs Darsie Hurlbutt, Hortense Shakley, Raymond Maths, and Doctor Maxman hastily undid their business clothing and took turns pressing themselves against the screen which quickly became smeary, though it was still possible to see Mrs Gustie Slovak's purple-and-coral-coloured lips parting, and pulsing across the screen at the other end.

There was a remote moment of complete satisfaction. It was the real thing.

Then Mrs Darsie Hurlbutt, Hortense Shakley, Raymond Maths, and Doctor Maxman fastened their business clothing. On-screen, Mrs Gustie Slovak pulled up her beige lace-effect shapewear, and pulled down her tweed-effect business skirt, rehooked her purple lace-effect bra, and rebuttoned her silk-effect blouse across her E-cup breasts and put on her tweed-effect business jacket.

Mrs Gustie Slovak said, *Do get back to us with the following required information's.*

*(1) YOUR FULL NAME* ..............................................
*(2) YOUR RESIDENTIAL ADDRESS*..................
*(3) YOUR POSTAL ADDRESS*...............................
*(4) YOUR PHONE AND FAX NUMBER*...............
*(5) YOUR E-MAIL ADDRESS*...............................
*(6) YOUR OCCUPATION*.........................................
*(7) YOUR OFFICIAL AGE*........................................

*(8) YOUR PHOTOGRAPH* ......................................
*(9) YOUR COUNTRY*.................................................
The meeting was closed.
The minutes of the meeting will be circulated.

## IX 1/2. Grow a Pair

It was about this time the cunt who owned the dick-bush noticed that one of her dicks was missing, so the witch (of course it was the witch. Who else grows dicks on a bush?) left her house, stopping only to put on a new, and particularly alluring bright blue strap-on, and set off to find the missing penis. She walked until she came to the city, her witch's nose high in the air, sniffing for the scent of sexual desire, but she could smell nothing but the odour of dirty washing.

The girl with the penis saw the witch as she got off a tram, recognised her immediately, and hurried in the other direction. The witch, scenting desire in her at once, followed, only to be distracted by a line of people queuing outside a large grey building that looked like an industrial shed, each clasping an object, from fire-tongs to flower pots, from bicycle pumps to ripe avocados.

As she walked away from her stop, the girl saw three big dicks climb off the tram at the front. This was pretty unusual, but she didn't stop. She could sense that the witch had spotted her, and was in a hurry to get away.

The three dicks had travelled into the city. They had taken the tram all the way to the main square, as they thought they might find the most pussy there. Already excited, and spilling a little at the tip due to rubbing up against other passengers, they got to their stop but, although it was lunchtime, they could find nowhere to eat. All the restaurants were shut, with signs in the windows like ANNUAL BREAK and CLOSED FOR REFURBISHMENT, though, glancing into the dusty interiors, there seemed to be no refurbishment going on. The only place that looked like it was open was a grey building, like an industrial shed, with a long line of people queuing outside the door, carrying objects from carrots to cut-glass wine goblets, from split pomegranates to flutes to cereal bowls. There seemed to be some kind of commotion going on inside.

As they shouldered through the crowds they caught sight of an enormous cunt, and they knew immediately that she was a witch. As soon as she stepped into the shed the massive machinery stopped. In the unexpected silence, the dicks heard the witch mumble a few words, saw her wave her magic dildo, and as soon as she did so, all the milk pans, and walking sticks, and poster tubes, and cushions, and champagne bottles and high-heeled pumps stopped spinning and whirring, and clattered to the ground. Then the people who had dropped all these things felt an itch in their crotches or sometimes in their chests, or even both. These were odd sensations that none of them had felt for a while, in fact not since they'd started using the machine. And when they investigated, they were surprised to find the itches were caused by tiny zippers they had never noticed before. Out of curiosity, of course they unzipped them and, when they did, out flopped perfect new sets of genitals, and no one was surprised or felt they had been given the wrong ones, and, of course they all wanted to test them out right away.

But this went on only for an afternoon, or perhaps it was a day, or maybe even a weekend. Who knows? It was a long time ago, anyway; people did things differently then. And after the orgy was over, some people went home happy and others caught diseases, some of which killed them, and still others were thrown out by their partners because, you know, life isn't a fairy tale.

The witch gave up looking for her missing dick – after all it was only regular-size – and she returned to her house in the suburbs accompanied by the three big dicks, who were really bigger than any she had seen before, and who, when not busy satisfying her needs, tended her dick-bushes by watering them every day.

And they all lived happily ever after.

The girl got home after wandering the streets. She was late, as she had taken the long way round, hoping the witch had not followed her. She got straight into bed, and Susana rolled over to the extreme limit of the mattress and wrapped herself in the sheet. She must have been balanced right on the edge. The dick pointed toward her, magnetised, and for a while we said nothing until finally Susana spoke.

'You know that I won't...' she said.

'Not even... once...?'

'No,' said Susana. 'Not even once.'

The penis drooped a little. But Susana was facing me now and she took the dick in her hands and began to pull it gently towards her, then stop, then the same thing again. It felt good with all those feelings that are usually on the inside transferred to the outside, like a glove turned inside out. And when I came, instead of the usual contracting and pulling in, there was a feeling of expanding and pushing out, like the dick wanted to fill all the space in the room. By the time I looked down it was already flaccid, and lay there resting in a little pool of gloop like an empty rubber thumb.

I knew right away that would be the only time I'd use it.

Susana moved in for good a couple of weeks later, and it seems to be going well. It's not much different from when we lived separately, which shows how much we were already living together. She never said anything more about my penis, which is an indicator of how great she is, and also how wise. I wasn't wearing it any more. I left it for a while on the sideboard but it got dusty and also a little flattened when I put a pile of books down on it without noticing. I tried to pull it back into shape but it never looked quite the same. I'm glad it was me that squashed it, not Susana. After all it was still my dick.

After this incident we discussed what we might do with it. Susana wanted to buy one of those old-style glass bell jars with flowers or wax fruit and put it on a stand in the hall but, still having proprietary feelings, I didn't want my dick to be always on display. We wrangled for a week and all the time the dick got dustier and once I thought we'd lost it altogether but I found it in the bottom of a bag of stuff I was going to take to Goodwill. It must have fallen in there from the sideboard. At least, I don't like to think about the alternative.

In the end we went to a tropical fish shop and bought a small aquarium, some coloured gravel, some water plants and one of those miniature castles made of cast resin. We kept the dick in there, and it was kind of a joke to see people do a double-take when they realised what it was, as it floated between the waterweeds, occasionally releasing a stream of tiny air bubbles from its tip.

Until one day it disappeared. It's possible that Alyssa's little dog, who jumped into the fish tank once during a visit, took it and ate it.

## Afterword: ...Into Fox

When the ex-IT Officer found herself falling down the cliff, she knew, somehow, that she was not dying, only falling. She knew this as soon as she was about halfway down and from that moment she began to relax and enjoy her fall. About three quarters of the way down, her body split and she became a large number of small, furry creatures, each no bigger than a teacup that, because of their inferior weight, did not reach a high enough terminal velocity to smash into the beach, but, when they landed, picked themselves up, shook the sand and pebbles out of their coats, and trotted off in a hundred different directions.

There were people who thought she'd transformed to escape sex, like those women capable of changing into reeds, into trees, into stars. But she knew there were always men who preferred to fuck knotholes, as well as those who sought out the tiny puffs of her furred vaginas. Warm bodies were all they wanted, and animals told no tales.

She chose wordlessness, and there were men who would come deep into the forest for it, even when she required difficult things of them. As for her furs, she had given them up for love or – no, that was wrong: for the opportunity to love, for a few minutes at least. The guys who came to the forest didn't stick around. After unclothing her, they left her asleep, taking her furs with them, trappers...

There were some men who wanted her to be all the animals of the forest, and that was just fine, until she visited the city and saw beautiful women, far more beautiful that her, walking by in her furs, on concrete pavements, reflected in department store windows.

## Acknowledgements

I wrote some of this in Whitstable at The Expansionists residency, hence the seaside flavour. Thank you, and thanks Tristram Burke, Katherine Angel, Lauren Elkin for conversations about sex. And all the people who've had sex with me.

## Joanna Walsh

Joanna Walsh's writing has been published by Dalkey (*Best European Fiction 2015*), *Granta*, Salt (*Best British Short Stories*, 2014 and 2015), and others. Her books include *Fractals* (2013, Blue Pavilion), *Hotel* (2015, Bloomsbury) and *Vertigo* (2015, Dorothy, A Publishing Project). She writes criticism for *The Guardian, The New Statesman* and *The National* (UAE). She is fiction editor at *3:AM Magazine*, and she runs #readwomen, described by the *New York Times* as 'a rallying cry for equal treatment for women writers.' She is also an illustrator.